PUFFIN BOOKS

ZOZU THE ROBOT

Rufus and Sarah found the Thing in the garden. It was like a ball, but it buzzed, changed colour, and *talked*, or anyway the thing inside it did. The Thing turns out to be Zozu the Robot, a tiny frightened metal creature, sent to Earth by his ruthless masters to solve the 'terrible question'. Rufus and Sarah get very fond of their little metal friend, and they even agree to return with him in his capsule to help prove that he has been telling the truth about humans. Little do they dream what an eerie world Zozu is taking them to, with its sinister Clever Clones and its threatening, terrifying, all-seeing Eye . . .

Diana Carter was born in London. She worked for some time in the film business and is the author of various novels. Having spent many years in Italy, she now lives in Surrey.

DIANA CARTER

Zozu the Robot

ILLUSTRATIONS BY
MIKE ROSE

PUFFIN BOOKS

Puffin Books, Penguin Books Ltd, Harmondsworth, Middlesex, England
Viking Penguin Inc., 40 West 23rd Street, New York, New York 10010, U.S.A.
Penguin Books Australia Ltd, Ringwood, Victoria, Australia
Penguin Books Canada Limited, 2801 John Street, Markham, Ontario, Canada L3R 1B4
Penguin Books (N.Z.) Ltd, 182–190 Wairau Road, Auckland 10, New Zealand

—

First published by Sidgwick & Jackson Ltd 1974
Published in Puffin Books 1976
Reprinted 1979, 1982, 1986

—

—

Printed and bound in Great Britain by
Cox & Wyman Ltd, Reading
Set in Monotype Ehrhardt

I

IT happened in the springtime.

Daffodils and tulips were blooming in the garden of the country cottage where Rufus lived with his sister, Sarah.

Rufus was older than Sarah and quite a lot taller. He had long legs and often wore a sticking plaster on one or the other of his knees. Although he was very good at doing head-over-heels and cartwheels on the lawn, Rufus sometimes fell off his bike.

Sarah, who had straight hair the colour of a conker and forget-me-not blue eyes, liked skipping and hide-and-seek.

On that April morning, the sun was shining brightly. Rufus and Sarah had a race to the end of the garden. He got there first, of course. Rufus always did.

'I've won,' he announced, squatting on his heels to stare at a patch of earth where, a week earlier, he'd planted some seeds.

'Come and look, Sarah. I think they're beginning to grow at last.'

But Sarah didn't move. She was staring at a blackcurrant bush at the edge of the vegetable garden.

'Rufus, there's a funny noise over here. A sort of buzzing.'

'It's just a bee, silly.'

'I am not silly. It's much too loud for a bee.'

Rufus went to the bush and listened too.

'That's funny.'

He bent to reach under the leaves. Then he gave a loud yell.

'Ow! It bit me.'

At that moment, something round rolled towards them and came to a stop right by Sarah's feet.

The buzzing, which sounded much louder now, was coming from right inside it. The strangest thing of all about this biting, buzzing object was that it exactly matched the colour of the earth on which it lay.

'What is it?' Sarah asked Rufus.

'I don't know. If it didn't buzz and if it wasn't that muddy colour, I'd say it was a ball.'

Cautiously, Rufus put out one finger and touched the thing.

'Ow!' he yelled again, snatching his finger away and putting it in his mouth. 'It doesn't bite. It stings.'

As he spoke, the extraordinary ball gave a hop and jumped straight out of the border and on to the lawn. The children watched in

astonishment as it became the same green as the grass around it.

'There must be a motor inside,' Rufus decided. 'Like my clockwork car. I expect it'll run down in a minute.'

'Where's the hole to put the key and wind it up?' asked Sarah.

'Underneath, I expect.'

'Look!' Sarah shouted. 'It's moving again.'

The thing, whatever it was, started to bowl across the lawn. It moved so fast that the children had to run to keep up with it. All three came to a stop beside Rufus's bike, a bright red two-wheeler. The side of the ball-thing which rested against the mudguard became red too.

'It keeps changing colour to match everything it touches,' exclaimed Sarah.

'Just like a chameleon,' said Rufus.

'Just like a what?'

'A chameleon. It's an animal, a kind of lizard that can change its colour. We saw them at the zoo. Don't you remember?'

'No, I don't. Do you think this ball can go any other colour? Let's try.'

'How?' asked Rufus. 'I'm not going to touch it any more, but you can if you like.'

Sarah was taking off her yellow cardigan.

'Put it on the end of a stick and wave it near the ball-thing.'

8

Rufus did as she suggested and, when one sleeve of the cardigan touched the ball, that part of it turned bright yellow.

'That's funny,' said Rufus. 'I've never seen a toy like this before.'

'Supposing it isn't a toy? Supposing it's something for grown-ups?'

'Look, Sarah. Look!' shouted Rufus.

The ball had begun to buzz much more loudly and, as Rufus pointed excitedly, a small window opened on its underside. Slowly, something that looked like a tiny crane unfolded itself from the window. It moved outwards and downwards. On the end of the crane arm there was a small scoop.

The children saw a furry caterpillar looping its way through the grass. Then, all of a sudden, the scoop snatched up the caterpillar and, before you could say 'Jack', let alone 'Robinson', the crane and its wildly wriggling prisoner had disappeared into the ball. The window clicked shut.

'Do you think it eats caterpillars?' Sarah asked in amazement.

'I don't know. Let's try to find it another one.'

While the children searched, the ginger cat, who lived in the next-door cottage, made himself thin enough to squeeze through his favourite gap in the hedge and he padded towards the ball. He studied it for a moment and then, bending low, curled out one paw to give it a playful tap.

The ball gave a loud HOOT and rolled quickly into the nearest flowerbed.

'I think,' said Sarah, 'that ball's afraid of Tizer.'

Rufus was carefully parting the leaves to look at the ball again. Sarah hung back a little.

'Perhaps it doesn't like being stared at.'

'Why ever not?'

'It's rude.'

'Don't be daft. It's only staring at people that's rude. How can a ball possibly mind?'

It was then that the most extraordinary thing of all happened.

The ball spoke!

2

A DEEP, deep voice which seemed to come from right inside the ball said very slowly, 'HOW . . . CAN . . . A . . . BALL . . . POSSIBLY . . . MIND ?'

Sarah was so astonished that she fell over backwards.

'Did you hear that, Rufus? It's talking!'

'That's not proper talking,' her brother jeered. 'It said the same thing I did.'

He glared rudely at the ball.

'Copycat!'

'COPYCAT!' repeated the ball.

Rufus stuck out his tongue.

'Can't you speak for yourself?'

'YES.'

'Well go on then. Say something.'

'YOU . . . FRIGHTEN . . . ME.'

'I'm awfully sorry,' Sarah apologized. 'We've never met a frightened ball before.'

'I . . . AM . . . NOT . . . A . . . BALL.'

'Well, what are you then?'

'I . . . AM . . . ZOZU . . . THE . . . ROBOT.'

'How do you do,' Sarah replied politely. 'We're Rufus and Sarah and you're in our garden you know.'

'IS . . . THIS . . . THE . . . PLANT . . . TEN?'

'What do you mean?' said Rufus. 'This is Lavender Cottage, Shepherd's Lane, Barton, Essex, England, The World. That's our proper address.'

'THE ... PLANT ... TEN ... IS ... THE ... END ... OF ... MY ... JOURNEY.'

'Have you come a long way?' asked Sarah.

'I ... HAVE ... BEEN ... TRAVELLING ... FOR ... A ... TRILLION ... DARK ... YEARS.'

'Golly!' exclaimed Rufus, very excited indeed. 'You don't mean ... You're not a spaceman, are you? I've always wanted to meet one.'

'I ... AM ... A ... ROBOT ... TRAVELLER.'

'Sarah, I think he must be a spaceman. Isn't it fantastic? He's come to visit the world and landed in our garden. Golly!' said Rufus again.

'But he thinks this is the plant ten.'

'So what? Maybe that's what they call the world where he comes from.'

Rufus knelt down and spoke encouragingly to the ball.

'What did you say your name was?'

'ZOZU ... THE ... ROBOT.'

'Well, listen, Zozu. I don't know if this is what you call the plant ten, but why don't you come out of the ball-thing and let us have a look at you?'

'I ... AM ... FRIGHTENED ... OF ... YOU ... MONSTERS.'

'Us? Monsters?' laughed Sarah. 'We're children.'

'WHAT ... ARE ... CHILDREN?'

'Well, they're ...' Rufus started. 'Oh, you
explain, Sarah.'

'Children are little people. Not grown-up, you
know.'

'I ... DO ... NOT ... KNOW,' said the voice.
'I ... WAS ... TOLD ... THAT ... THE ...
CREATURES ... OF ... THE ... PLANT ... TEN
... WOULD ... NOT ... BE ... BIGGER ...
THAN ... THE ... WILD ... ANIMAL ... I ...
CAPTURED.'

'What's he talking about?' Rufus asked Sarah.

'I suppose he means the caterpillar. The one
he pulled into the ball.'

'THIS ... ANIMAL ... DOES ... NOT ...
TALK ... LIKE ... YOU.'

'Of course it doesn't. Everyone knows that
caterpillars can't speak.'

'THEN ... YOU ... ARE ... THE ... MOST
... CLEVER ... ANIMALS ... ON ... THIS ...
PLANT?'

'Yes,' said Rufus thoughtfully. 'I suppose we
are. We talk and we build things and we can do
sums.'

He gave Sarah a nasty look.

'At least, some of us can. So we must be more
clever than all the animals put together.'

'THERE...HAS...BEEN...A...MISTAKE.
I ... DID ... NOT ... EXPECT ... SUCH ...
HUGE ... MONSTERS.'

'Who are you?' asked Rufus. 'And why have
you come here?'

'I ... HAVE ... BEEN ... BORROWED ... BY
... THE ... PLANT ... SIX ... TO ... DIS-
COVER ... THE ... ANSWER ... TO ... THE ...
TERRIBLE ... QUESTION ... AND ... THIS ...
IS ... MY ... FIRST ... MISSION.'

'Won't you please come out of the ball, Zozu?'
pleaded Sarah. 'We promise not to hurt you.'

'I ... AM ... AFRAID. YOU ... ARE ... SO ...
ENORMOUS ... AND ... THIS ... PLANT ...
IS ... FULL ... OF ... FIERCE ... MONSTERS.'

'Don't be scared. We'll look after you.'

'WHAT ... ABOUT ... THE ... BEAST ...
WITH ... KNIVES ... ON ... ITS ... FEET?'

Sarah was puzzled.

'What's he talking about, Rufus?'

'I think he must mean Tizer. Those aren't
knives, Zozu. They're claws. Tizer's hardly more
than a kitten. He just wanted to play. Anyway,
he's gone now, so it's quite safe. Honestly.'

'THEN ... I ... WILL ... COME ... OUT.'

3

RUFUS and Sarah knelt down to get a better view of the ball. They heard a whirring noise and saw a door, about the size and shape of an egg, open upwards. Then a small flight of stairs unfolded gradually until the bottom step touched the ground.

A tiny figure appeared in the door. It was hard to see clearly because he was the same colour as the ball.

Zozu began to move down the steps, very slowly and very stiffly.

The first thing Sarah saw was that, instead of feet, he walked on two metal discs which reminded her of the saucers in her dolls' tea set. Zozu's head was the same shape as an ice-cream cone, but upside down. Two quivering feelers sprouted from the top. His arms and legs, which were thin and shiny, seemed to be joined at the knees and elbows with little screws. Each hand had seven fingers.

Zozu had one eye in the front of his cone-shaped head and another in the back. His mouth looked like the slot in a letter-box. The robot's body was square and covered all over with flashing lights, switches, buttons, and knobs.

'Your front's just like the dashboard of Daddy's car,' said Rufus critically.

'Don't be so nasty,' Sarah told him. 'I think it looks very smart with all those red and green lights going on and off all the time,' she added kindly to Zozu. 'Can I pick you up?'

'NOT...FAST...PLEASE...I...HAVE... NO...HEAD...FOR...HEIGHTS.'

Sarah held the robot's body gently between her thumb and first finger.

'Don't forget,' Rufus ordered. 'Ever so slowly. We don't want him to feel sick.'

Sarah took as long as she could to bring Zozu level with her face. She stared at the robot and the robot stared back at her. As Zozu had no eyelid, Sarah was the first to blink.

'Does everybody look like you where you come from?' asked Rufus.

'ONLY...EXPLORERS...WHO...ARE... MADE...SO...THEY...CAN...LIVE... ANYWHERE.'

'If you took a trillion dark years to get here, you must be awfully old,' said Sarah.

'WHAT...IS...OLD?'

'Our Grandpa's old,' said Rufus. 'He's sixty-five.'

'Zozu, why do you speak so jerkily?' asked Sarah.

'I...CAN...USE...MY...ELECTRIC

... BRAIN ... TO ... SPEAK ... ANY ...
LANGUAGE ... BUT ... IT ... TAKES ...
TIME ... TO ... FIND ... EACH ... WORD.'

'And why have you got one eye at the front
and the other at the back?' Rufus queried.

'TO ... SEE ... ALL ... ROUND ... OF ...
COURSE.'

'My Mummy's always saying she needs eyes
in the back of her head,' Sarah said. 'Why did
you come here, Zozu?'

'TO ... HELP ... ANSWER ... THE ...
TERRIBLE ... QUESTION,' Zozu replied. 'BUT
... I ... MUST ... HAVE ... LANDED ... IN
... THE ... WRONG ... PLACE. NOTHING ...
IS ... THE ... WAY ... THEY ... TOLD ... ME
... IT ... WOULD ... BE.'

'So what are you going to do now?'

'I ... MUST ... ASK ... MY ... MASTERS,'
said Zozu. 'THEY ... MAY ... ORDER ... ME ...
TO ... FIND ... OUT ... ABOUT ... THIS ...
PLACE ... AND ... REPORT ... TO ... PLANT
... SIX. BUT ... I ... AM ... AFRAID.'

'I don't blame you,' said Sarah sympathetic-
ally. 'Seeing us must have come as a nasty
shock.'

'YOU ... DO ... NOT ... UNDERSTAND.
A ... WELL ... MADE ... ROBOT ... IS ...
NEVER ... AFRAID ... OF ... ANYTHING.
THERE ... MUST ... HAVE ... BEEN ... A ...

MISTAKE ... IN ... THE ... FACTORY. I ...
AM ... A ... BAD ... ROBOT. IF ... MY ...
MASTERS ... FIND ... OUT ... THEY ...
WILL ... SCRAP ... ME.'

'How mean!' exclaimed Sarah. 'I'm often
scared. And Rufus is sometimes too, even though
he's two years older than I am.'

Rufus was indignant. 'When?'

'What about the time we played hide-and-
seek and you were shut in the garage? You were
frightened then, weren't you?'

'That was your fault. You gave up too easily.
If Mummy hadn't found me, I'd have been there
for ages.'

Rufus didn't want Sarah to tell Zozu that he'd
cried, so he quickly asked the robot another
question.

'Where have you come from?'

'EARTH,' said Zozu mysteriously.

Then, before Rufus could ask what he meant,
the robot's back eye fixed on the cottage.

'WHAT ... IS ... THAT?'

'Our house. Would you like to meet Mummy?
She's in the kitchen.'

'IS ... MUMMY ... BIG ... TOO?'

'Much bigger than we are,' said Sarah. 'The
top of my head just comes up to her waist. But
she's very nice. You'll see.'

Zozu gave a sort of gasp. The lights on his

chest began to flash faster and faster until all the red ones went out and the robot turned bright green.

'I ... AM ... FRIGHTENED. PLEASE ... DO ... NOT ... SHOW ... ME ... TO ... THE ... MUMMY ... GIANT.'

'Then we'd better not let any of the grown-ups see you,' Rufus decided. 'You'll be our secret. Mine and Sarah's.'

'We'll take care of you,' Sarah added.

'Zozu?' asked Rufus thoughtfully, 'Why do you change colour like that?'

'IT ... IS ... LESS ... DANGEROUS.'

'Well, it does make you difficult to see. But why did you go all green just now?'

'BECAUSE ... OF ... THE ... MISTAKE ... IN ... THE ... ROBOT ... FACTORY,' said Zozu. 'EVERY ... TIME ... I ... AM ... FRIGHTENED ... I ... GO ... GREEN.'

'How horrid for you,' sympathized Sarah. 'Can't you do anything about it?'

'I ... MUST ... TELL ... MY ... MASTERS,' said Zozu. 'I ... EXPECT ... THEY ... WILL ... CALL ... ME ... BACK ... TO ... EARTH ... IMMEDIATELY.'

'Do you have to tell them?' Rufus asked. 'We'd love you to stay, wouldn't we, Sarah?'

'Do try, Zozu. Supposing we help you answer this terrible question? Wouldn't they be pleased?

'WILL ... YOU ... REALLY ... HELP ...
ME ?'

Both children nodded.

'THEN ... I ... WILL ... TELL ... THEM
... ABOUT ... THIS ... PECULIAR ... PLANT
... AND ... SEE ... WHAT ... THEY ... SAY.'

'Super,' grinned Rufus.

'PUT ... ME ... DOWN ... PLEASE.'

When Sarah had lowered Zozu gently to the
foot of the steps, he clanked stiffly up them and
disappeared inside the ball.

Rufus and Sarah crossed fingers for luck and
waited.

4

SEVERAL minutes passed. Then Zozu reappeared in the little egg-shaped doorway.

'I ... AM ... TO ... STAY.'

Rufus and Sarah uncrossed their fingers and
grinned delightedly.

'MY ... MASTERS ... WANT ... ME ... TO
... EXPLORE ... THIS ... PLANT,' said Zozu.
'THEY ... BELIEVE ... THE ... ANSWER ...
TO ... THE ... TERRIBLE ... QUESTION ...
CAN ... BE ... FOUND ... HERE ... AND ... I
... AM ... TO ... CONTINUE ... WITH ...
MISSION ... ONE.'

'We'll help you explore,' said Sarah.

'But how are we going to carry him around?'
wondered Rufus.

'What about his ball?' suggested Sarah.

'Don't be daft. Any grown-up who saw a ball
that kept changing colour like that would be
bound to ask all kinds of questions. Anyway, it
prickles.'

'WHAT ... IS ... A ... BALL?' asked Zozu.

'Don't you know?' said a surprised Rufus.
'Hang on a minute and I'll show you. Where's
yours, Sarah?'

She frowned, trying to remember.

'I think it's in the garage.'

Long-legged Rufus was half-way there when she called after him, 'And mind you don't get locked in again.'

Soon Rufus was back carrying a white ball decorated with red spots.

'That's a ball,' he told Zozu.

'WHAT ... DOES ... IT ... DO?'

'It bounces,' said Rufus, showing him. 'And you can play games with it like pig-in-the-middle. Only Sarah and I can't play that because you need three people. Anyway she's a butter-fingers.'

The two feelers that sprouted from the top of Zozu's head quivered so much that they all became tangled up and he had to use his fourteen fingers to free them.

'WHAT ... IS ... BUTTERFINGERS? MY ... ELECTRIC ... BRAIN ... DOES ... NOT ... UNDERSTAND.'

'It means someone who can't catch a ball,' Rufus explained.

'THANK ... YOU,' said Zozu. 'NOW ... TELL ... ME. IF ... MY ... MATTER ... MACHINE ... LOOKED ... LIKE ... THE ... BALL ... COULD ... YOU ... HELP ... ME ... EXPLORE ... WITHOUT ... SHOWING ... ME ... TO THE ... MUMMY ... GIANT?'

'Yes,' said Rufus. 'As long as you stayed

23

inside it. Mummy's used to seeing us with the ball. We often play with it.'

'THEN ... FIRST ... I ... WILL ... MAKE ... MY ... MATTER ... MACHINE ... SAFE ... FOR ... YOU ... TO ... TOUCH.'

As he spoke, Zozu pulled one of the switches on his flashing chest.

'IT ... DOES ... NOT ... STING ... NOW.'

Rufus touched it just to make sure.

'I wish you'd done that right in the beginning,' he said crossly. 'It was just like a nettle before.'

'NOW,' instructed the robot, 'PUT ... THE ... BALL ... CLOSE ... TO ... THE ... MATTER ... MACHINE ... AND ... STAND ... BACK.'

Rufus did as Zozu asked and he and Sarah retreated to a safe distance.

The matter machine began to hum louder than ever and gave off a strange smell which made Sarah sneeze. When the humming stopped, the matter machine was white all over.

'What about the spots?' asked Rufus.

In reply Zozu pushed a button which would have been under his chin if he'd had a chin.

Slowly but surely the matter machine broke out in scarlet spots, just like the ones on Sarah's ball.

It reminded Rufus of the time they'd both had the measles.

'That's clever,' Sarah said admiringly.

'We'll have to hide the real ball,' Rufus decided. 'Otherwise, Mummy might wonder why we suddenly have two of them.'

'I know,' said Sarah. 'Hide it in the box by the front gate where Mr Simpkins puts the milk. Mummy won't look in there again until to-morrow morning. You see,' she explained to Zozu, 'we have to hide the bottles, otherwise the bluetits peck through the tops and drink all the cream.'

'Good idea,' said Rufus. 'I'll go.'

While Rufus was away, Sarah asked Zozu if he'd feel sick, being carried around in the matter machine.

'I always do in our car,' she added.

'ROBOTS ... NEVER ... FEEL ... SICK,' the robot told her.

'Lucky them,' Sarah said enviously as Rufus returned. 'Now. Where shall we explore first?'

The robot pointed to the cottage again.

'THERE.'

'All right. But remember to stay in the matter machine until we say it's safe to come out.'

'I ... WILL ... REMEMBER.'

The robot disappeared from the egg-shaped doorway, the tiny staircase folded up and into the matter machine, and the opening whirred shut.

No one could possibly have known that Zozu

and his machine were anything more than a perfectly ordinary ball.

Rufus went to pick it up.

'Let me,' said Sarah. 'It's my ball.'

'No, it isn't,' Rufus pointed out. 'It belongs to Zozu. So we'll take it in turns.'

'Then I bags first turn.'

'Oh, all right,' said Rufus sulkily. 'But mind how you carry it. We don't want him to be sick.'

Sarah tucked the machine under her arm.

'Robots,' she said importantly, 'are never sick. So there!'

5

RUFUS and Sarah went into the cottage by the back door which led directly into the kitchen. Their mother was standing by the sink, peeling potatoes.

'Finished playing already?' she asked. 'Lunch won't be ready for another half an hour yet.'

'I'm thirsty, Mummy,' said Sarah. 'Can I have a drink of water?'

'Of course. Here's a glass.'

Sarah put the matter machine on the draining board and turned on the cold tap. Just as the glass was nearly full, the matter machine rolled down the draining board and fell into the sink among the potato peelings.

'Do be careful, Sarah,' yelled Rufus. 'You'll get him . . . I mean it, dirty.'

Rufus's mother turned to stare at him.

'What a funny thing to say about a ball. Are you feeling all right, Rufus?'

Luckily, their mother now had her back to the sink. So she didn't see the tiny crane arm appear from the side of the matter machine, or the little scoop which snatched up a piece of potato peeling and whisked it inside.

'Don't do that,' Sarah said loudly.

Her mother gave Sarah a puzzled look.

'Don't do what, Sarah? Really, I don't know what on earth's the matter with you two today.'

Both children thought this was very funny and started to giggle.

Between giggles, Rufus sang, 'Oh dear, what can the matter be? Oh dear, what can the matter be?'

Sarah joined in, 'Oh dear, what can the matter be? Zozu's so long at the fair.'

'Who's so long at the fair?' asked her mother.

'She meant Johnny,' Rufus said quickly. 'Sarah always gets the words wrong.' He glared at his sister. 'Don't you?'

For once, Sarah didn't argue. She just nodded.

'Well, I must get on. Otherwise lunch'll be terribly late. So take that ball out of the sink one of you and let me finish the potatoes.'

'Let's go upstairs,' said Rufus, picking up the matter machine.

When he and Sarah reached the room they shared, he put it carefully on the table.

'You,' he said crossly to Sarah, 'nearly gave the game away. And after you promised, too.'

'I didn't mean to, honestly. I'm terribly sorry, Zozu,' Sarah said to the matter machine.

Rufus added, 'It's all right. You can come out now, Zozu.'

The egg-shaped door opened and Zozu stood

at the top of the steps. He was bright green all over.

'There!' exclaimed Rufus. 'He's frightened and it's all your fault, Sarah.'

'IT ... IS ... NOT ... SARAH'S ... FAULT.' said Zozu. 'I ... AM ... FRIGHTENED ... OF ... THE ... MUMMY ... GIANT. SHE ... MUST ... BE ... THE ... BIGGEST ... ON ... THE ... WHOLE ... PLANT.'

'Mummy?' laughed Sarah. 'She isn't very tall. You should see our Uncle Ken. He's six feet two inches tall.'

'DO ... NOT ... LET ... ME ... SEE ... THE ... UNCLE ... KEN ... GIANT,' said Zozu. 'I ... MIGHT ... BLOW ... A ... FUSE ... WITH ... FRIGHT.'

'Then we won't,' said Sarah. 'But you were very naughty in the kitchen, Zozu. Supposing Mummy had seen you taking that piece of potato peeling?'

'Is that what he did?' asked Rufus. 'Sarah's right. You mustn't do it again, Zozu.'

The robot hung his head in shame.

Sarah felt sorry for him.

'Would you like a piece of chocolate?' she asked.

'WHAT ... IS ... CHOCOLATE?'

'This.'

She showed him a square she had saved.

'WHAT . . . DO . . . YOU . . . DO . . . WITH . . .
IT ?'

'You eat it, of course, silly,' said Rufus.

Sarah offered Zozu the chocolate. Then,
seeing that the square was nearly as big as his
chest, she broke off a tiny piece with her thumb-
nail.

'It's fruit and nut,' Sarah explained.

'HOW . . . DO . . . YOU . . . EAT . . . IT ?'

'Put it in your mouth and chew.'

'WHAT . . . IS . . . MY . . . MOUTH ?'

Rufus pointed to the letter-box slot under
Zozu's front eye.

'There.'

All the green lights on Zozu's chest went out
and the red ones flashed at an alarming rate.
Quite soon he was completely scarlet.

'What's the matter, Zozu? Are you ill or
something?'

'NO,' said the robot. 'I . . . AM . . . DOING . . .
WHAT . . . YOU . . . CALL . . . LAUGHING.'

'But why?' asked Rufus.

'I . . . WILL . . . SHOW . . . YOU. ASK . . . ME
. . . A . . . VERY . . . DIFFICULT . . . QUESTION.'

Rufus thought hard.

Then he clapped his hands.

'I know. What's six times eight?'

'SIX . . . TIMES . . . EIGHT ?' repeated Zozu,
pulling a lever on his chest.

31

Almost immediately, a very small piece of paper shot out of his mouth.

'READ ... THE ... ANSWER ... RUFUS ... GIANT.'

Rufus looked at the paper.

'It says forty-eight.'

'Is that the right answer?' Sarah asked her brother.

Rufus muttered, 'Three eights are twenty-four, four eights are thirty-two, five eights are forty, six eights are ... yes! Forty-eight. Golly, how clever you are, Zozu.'

'Can you answer other kinds of questions, too?' Sarah wondered.

'ANYTHING ... EXCEPT ... ONE ... QUESTION ... THE ... TERRIBLE ... QUESTION ... OF ... PLANT ... SIX.'

'And don't you ever eat?' asked Rufus.

Zozu turned bright red again and the lights on his chest flashed so fast they made Sarah blink.

'He's laughing at you again,' she told her brother.

'ROBOTS ... DO ... NOT ... NEED ... TO ... EAT.'

'Never ever?' said Rufus, amazed.

'NEVER ... EVER,' the robot repeated.

'Would you like to meet our pet mouse?' Sarah asked. 'We call him Mister Pink because of his eyes. He lives in a cage with a wheel and sometimes he runs round and round in the wheel for ages and ages.'

'ANOTHER ... GIANT ?'

Zozu began to get a little green.

'No, he's quite small,' Rufus said, fetching the mouse's cage from the windowsill. 'Look.'

Zozu turned very green indeed as he stared at Mister Pink, who was snowy white except for his eyes, which were – as Sarah had already explained – pink.

Poor Zozu developed a terrible stutter.

'MMY ... ELECTRIC ... BBBRAIN ... THTHINKS ... THTHIS ... MMMONSTER ... CCAN ... ANSWER ... PPPART ... OF ... THE ... TTTTERRIBLE ... QUQUESTION. I ... MMMUST ... TTTAKE ... HIM ... WWWITH ... MMME ... TTTO ... PPPLANT ... SIX.'

6

Rufus was horrified.

'You can't take Mister Pink to plant six, Zozu. He belongs to us.'

'AND ... YYOU ... ARE ... NNOT ... AFRAID ... OF ... TTHIS ... MMMONSTER?'

'Of course not,' Rufus declared, taking the mouse out of his cage and stroking him.

'DDOES ... IT ... DDO ... THIS ... THING ... CALLED ... EATING?'

Rufus returned Mister Pink to his cage.

'Mostly he has rice and breadcrumbs soaked in milk.'

'Sometimes he has a bit of cake,' added Sarah.

'MY ... ELECTRIC ... BRAIN ... TELLS ... ME ... THAT ... IT ... COULD ... BE ... PART ... OF ... THE ... ANSWER ... TO ... THE ... TERRIBLE ... QUESTION.'

'I do wish you'd tell us what this question is,' said Rufus irritably.

'IT ... IS ... TOO ... DIFFICULT,' said Zozu. 'TELL ... ME ... MORE ... ABOUT ... THIS ... PLANT.'

'What do you want to know?' asked Sarah.

'DO ... YOU ... HAVE ... A ... WHITE ... COLD ... HERE?'

The children tried to work out what Zozu meant. It was Rufus who solved the riddle first.

'Snow! That's white and cold. It's lovely to play in.'

'WHERE ... CAN ... I ... SEE ... THIS ... SNOW ?'

'You can't. We only have it in winter. It's spring now,' said Sarah.

'But in some places they have it all the time,' Rufus explained.

'WHERE ?'

'Right at the very top of the world and right at the very bottom. I'll show you.'

Rufus fetched a picture book from the shelf and turned the pages until he came to one that showed Eskimo children playing outside a little house made completely of snow.

'Their house is called an igloo,' Rufus told the robot.

'WHY ... DO ... THOSE ... CHILDREN ... GIANTS ... WEAR ... THE ... SKINS ... OF ... OTHER ... ANIMALS ?'

'To keep them warm. They wear the fur side inside and the skin side outside. My Mummy knows a poem about that,' said Rufus. 'But it's very long and I can't remember it any more. Look, Zozu, here's another picture. It shows you the animals that live in those places.'

The little robot stared at the polar bears and penguins with his front eye for a long time.

'YES,' he said finally. 'THAT . . . IS . . . THE . . . WHITE . . . COLD. I . . . MUST . . . TAKE . . . IT . . . BACK . . . TO . . . PLANT . . . SIX . . . TOO.'

Sarah gave a little sigh.

'But we already told you, Zozu. There isn't any here now.'

Zozu used one of his fourteen fingers to point at the picture.

'THEN . . . WHAT . . . IS . . . THAT ?'

'It's only a drawing,' said Rufus, turning another page of the book. 'Here's a picture of the whole world. We live on that squiggly island that's coloured brown. The Eskimoes and the polar bears live right up there in the bit that's covered in white.'

'THEN . . . WE . . . ARE . . . VERY . . . NEAR . . . THE . . . TOP . . . OF . . . THE . . . BALL . . . YOU . . . CALL . . . WHOLE . . . WORLD.'

'But the world isn't like that really,' said Rufus. 'Somebody drew a picture so that you could see it all at once. The world's enormous.'

'I . . . DO . . . NOT . . . UNDERSTAND.'

The two feelers sprouting from the top of Zozu's head became tangled again.

'Oh dear,' said Sarah. 'You are in a muddle, aren't you?'

Rufus thought hard.

Then he said, 'Listen, Zozu. Our school's on the other side of the village. It takes us ten minutes to walk there. Now I'll draw you a picture of our house and our school.'

Rufus took a crayon and a piece of paper from a drawer.

'See?' he asked, drawing quickly. 'That's our house.'

'You forgot the chimney,' said Sarah.

Rufus added one.

'And here,' he told Zozu, 'is our school.'

'It has many more windows than that,' Sarah announced. 'And why do you always stick your tongue out when you draw?'

'Do I?' Rufus asked in surprise. 'I never noticed.'

He turned the picture the right way up for Zozu.

'That's a drawing of our house and our school. But if I started to walk to school now it would still take ten minutes to get there.'

'Not if Daddy drove you in the car,' said Sarah. 'That way it hardly takes any time at all.'

The green lights on Zozu's chest went out and he turned red all over.

'Rufus,' said Sarah. 'He's laughing at us again.'

'What's so funny, Zozu?' asked Rufus crossly.

'NOW . . . I . . . UNDERSTAND.'

'Understand what?'

But, before the robot could begin to explain, Rufus and Sarah heard their mother calling, 'Come on, children. Lunch is ready.'

'Shall we take the matter machine downstairs with us?' Sarah asked her brother.

'I ... WOULD ... LIKE ... TO ... STAY ... HERE ... WITH ... THE ... PICTURE ... BOOK,' said Zozu.

'Are you sure you won't be frightened all on your own?'

'I ... AM ... SURE.'

'Come on, Sarah,' urged Rufus. 'I'm hungry!'

7

RUFUS felt much less hungry after he'd eaten three fish fingers and a big helping of golden, crispy chips.

There was strawberry jelly to follow.

Sarah was just about to eat her last spoonful when she suddenly sat bolt upright and said, 'Nineteen times twenty-two.'

Her mother laughed.

'And I thought you were the one who didn't like arithmetic?'

'I don't. I hate it,' Sarah agreed. 'But that's the most difficult question I can think of.'

'It certainly isn't easy,' said her mother. 'But why are you trying to think up difficult questtions?'

'Because . . .' started Sarah.

Rufus kicked her under the table.

'It's just a game we were playing upstairs,' he mumbled.

Sarah kicked him back.

'Do you know the answer, Mummy?'

'Not just like that. I'd have to work it out with a pencil and paper.'

'We've got a friend who could do it in his head ever so quickly,' Sarah told her proudly.

'Then he or she must be very clever,' said her mother. 'Is it anyone I know?'

Rufus said quickly, 'No, it isn't. Can we get down now, Mummy? We want to go back to our game.'

'Down you get then. I'll call you when it's television time.'

Rufus pushed back his chair.

'Oh,' he said airily, 'I 'spect we'll be much too busy to watch soppy old telly today.'

His mother looked astonished.

'My goodness. Then it must be an exciting game.'

'It isn't a game,' Sarah chimed in. 'It's the most . . .'

Before she could add another word, Rufus grabbed Sarah by the hand and pulled her out of the kitchen.

'You,' he whispered, as they climbed the stairs to their room, 'nearly gave the game away. Can't you ever keep a secret?'

'Of course I can,' said an indignant Sarah. 'I was only going to say that it's the most exciting real thing that's ever happened.'

'Just like a girl,' Rufus grumbled.

Sarah ran into their room ahead of him.

'Zozu, I've thought of a very difficult question for your electric brain.'

Then, looking dismayed, she turned to Rufus.

'The matter machine! It's gone.'

'Maybe it rolled off the table,' suggested Rufus, going on his hands and knees to look.

But the matter machine wasn't under the table or under the bottom bunk-bed or under any of the other pieces of furniture.

It was nowhere to be seen.

Sarah started to cry.

'He's gone. We've lost Zozu.'

While Rufus was searching high and low for the matter machine, he noticed something else.

The mouse cage was empty.

'And where's Mister Pink? He can't have escaped. The door of his cage is shut.'

Sarah wailed, 'Zozu's gone home and he's taken Mister Pink with him, just as he said.'

Rufus put his arm round her shoulders.

'Don't cry, Sarah. Zozu must have been bored all on his own. But I do think it was rude of him not to say good-bye.'

Sarah gave a big sniff.

'Poor Mister Pink. I bet Zozu won't remember to feed him.'

Rufus had a sudden idea.

'Zozu can't have taken Mister Pink, Sarah.'

'Why not? He wanted to take him, didn't he?'

'Because Mister Pink's too big to go through the door of the matter machine.'

Sarah brightened.

'I didn't think of that. But I've thought of something else.'

'What?'

'Zozu isn't tall enough to open the door of the cage. And anyway he was scared of Mister Pink, remember?'

'Let's have a proper look.'

But, although they searched absolutely everywhere, the children couldn't find their pet mouse.

'I give up,' said Sarah, slumping miserably at the table.

Then she said to her brother, 'Rufus? Did you put the picture book away?'

'You know I didn't. Zozu said he wanted to look at it some more.'

'Well, where is it?'

'On the table where I left it, I suppose.'

'It isn't. That's vanished too.'

'Then Zozu must have borrowed it.'

'Without asking? It's a bit mean.'

'Do you know what I think,' said Rufus slowly, 'I think Zozu's borrowed Mister Pink and the book.'

'But how could he? They were both too big.'

Rufus stared at the open window.

'I tell you what, Sarah,' he said in a dreamy,

far-away voice, 'Zozu's flown away. He's gone to where the Eskimoes and the polar bears live. He's gone to find some snow, just as he said.'

Rufus gave a little smile.

'And I bet you anything you like he'll be back again.'

8

THE afternoon passed very slowly.

Sarah and Rufus tried to play but it wasn't any fun. They kept thinking about Zozu and wondering if the little robot would ever return.

Instead of watching television, they gazed out of their bedroom window. Later, when they went downstairs for supper, neither was hungry.

By bedtime the sky was navy blue all over. The only light came from a small slice of new moon, rising over the trees in the front garden.

Sadly, Rufus leaned out of the window.

'He'll never manage to find his way now.'

His mother came into the room, carrying two pairs of clean pyjamas.

'Come on, children,' she said briskly. 'Time to get undressed. Shut the window please, Rufus.'

'Oh, Mummy. Can't we have it open? Just a tiny bit?' pleaded Sarah.

'It's awfully hot in here,' Rufus added.

'Well, just a bit then. Do hurry up. Daddy'll be home any minute and he'll expect to find you both in bed.'

Rufus and Sarah took it in turns to sleep in

the top bunk. Sleeping there was more fun because you had to climb a ladder to get in and out of bed.

This week it was Sarah's turn.

She reached the top of the ladder just as her father came upstairs.

'Hello, you two,' he said, smiling. 'Had a nice day?'

'Some of it was and some of it wasn't,' said Rufus. 'We lost a ball.'

'That was silly of you. I do wish you'd learn to take more care of your toys.'

Sarah snuggled under the bedclothes.

'Tell us about spacemen, Daddy.'

'What do you want to know?'

'Have you ever met one?'

'Not to speak to. But I've seen them on television. So have you. Don't you remember when we saw them walking about on the moon?'

Rufus said, 'She doesn't mean that kind. She means spacemen from other plants.'

His father chuckled.

'Not plants, Rufus. Planets.'

'Has one ever come to earth before?'

'From another planet? Not as far as we know.'

'Is the moon a very long way away, Daddy?' Sarah wanted to know.

'A very, very long way. About two hundred thousand miles.'

'And those men we saw bouncing around,' Sarah went on. 'Did they find any little robots?'

'What an idea!' exclaimed her father. 'All they found were rocks and dust. There's no life of any kind on the moon.'

'It sounds very boring,' Rufus commented. 'But what about other places in space? Are there people and robots there?'

'We just don't know yet,' said his father. 'Scientists in Russia and America have been trying to find out more about Mars and Venus by sending spacecraft filled with instruments. But the most likely places to find other creatures anything like ourselves are millions and millions of miles away in outer space.'

'A trillion dark years,' Sarah said to herself, remembering what Zozu had said.

'Supposing someone from outer space came to visit us,' said Rufus. 'What would we do?'

'That would depend,' his father said slowly.

'On what?'

'All sorts of things, Rufus. For a start it would depend on whether we could talk to them or not. Then it would depend on whether they were friends or enemies. Visitors from space might be a very strange shape, something we can't even begin to imagine.'

'And if they were friendly and we could talk to them. What would we do then?'

'Well,' said his father, thinking hard. 'I suppose they'd be much more clever than we are because we're only just beginning to learn about space travel. So we'd probably turn them over to our best scientists to find out everything they could.'

'That doesn't sound like much fun for them,' muttered Sarah.

'Visitors from space might be very frightening,' her father said. 'For instance, they could be huge giants.'

'And they might be teeny weeny robots who were frightened of everyone except children,' added Rufus.

His father laughed.

'You could be right. Time you both went to sleep. Do you want me to shut the window?'

At that very moment a white ball decorated with red spots whooshed through the window, landed on the carpet, bounced twice and rolled under the table.

'What on earth ...?' said the children's father, bending to pick it up. 'Is this the ball you lost?'

'That's the one,' said Rufus, grinning.

'Someone must have found it and thrown it in. How kind of him. I'll put it away in the toy cupboard.'

'No, don't do that, Daddy. Leave it on the table where we can see it,' pleaded Rufus.

'All right. But take good care of it now. You might not be so lucky again. Good night, Rufus. Good night, Sarah. Sleep well.'

'Night, night, Daddy,' the children chorused, as he switched off the light and closed the door.

As soon as they were alone, Rufus whispered, 'Sarah?'

'Yes?'

'Zozu's back!'

9

SARAH started to clamber out of the top
bunk.

'Hang on a minute,' Rufus ordered. 'Wait
till I turn on the light or you'll fall off the ladder.
We must be very quiet.'

The little egg-shaped door of the matter
machine was already open when the children
could see clearly again. Zozu stood at the top of
the steps.

'We thought you'd gone home without saying
good-bye,' said Sarah.

'*I* didn't,' corrected Rufus. 'I said he'd come
back, didn't I? But where have you been,
Zozu?'

'I ... WENT ... TO ... EXPLORE ... THE ...
TOP ... OF ... THIS ... PLANT ... AND ...
COLLECT ... SOME ... WHITE ... COLD.'

'Just what I said, Sarah. But how are you going
to stop the snow melting, Zozu?' Rufus wanted
to know.

'I ... HAVE ... PUT ... IT ... IN ... MY ...
STAY ... SAME ... MACHINE.'

'What's that?' asked Sarah.

'JUST ... WHAT ... IT ... SAYS,' Zozu told
her. 'ANYTHING ... IN ... THE ... STAY ...

SAME ... MACHINE ... STAYS ... THE ... SAME.'

'For always?'

'FOR ... AS ... LONG ... AS ... I ... NEED ... IT.'

'Where's Mister Pink?' demanded Sarah. 'And our big picture book?'

'THEY ... ARE ... IN ... THE ... MATTER ... MACHINE.'

'Why?' asked Rufus.

'PLANT ... SIX ... WANTS ... TO ... SEE ... THE ... WHITE ... MONSTER ... WITH ... PINK ... EYES,' said Zozu. 'AND ... I ... NEEDED ... THE ... PICTURE ... BOOK ... TO ... FIND ... MY ... WAY.'

'But how did they get in there? They're both too big to go through the door.'

'I ... USED ... MY ... GET ... SMALL ... MACHINE ... WHICH ... I ... SHALL ... USE ... ON ... YOU ... TOO.'

'On us! Whatever for?'

'PLANT ... SIX ... REFUSES ... TO ... BELIEVE ... THAT ... YOU ... ARE ... AS ... BIG ... AS ... I ... SAY,' Zozu explained. 'THEY ... SAY ... I ... AM ... A ... LYING ... ROBOT ... AND ... MY ... MASTERS ... WILL ... SCRAP ... ME ... WHEN ... I ... GET ... BACK ... TO ... EARTH.'

'That isn't fair,' Rufus exclaimed.

'PLEASE . . . COME . . . WITH . . . ME . . . TO
. . . PLANT . . . SIX. THEN . . . THEY . . . WILL
. . . KNOW . . . I . . . AM . . . TELLING . . . THE
. . . TRUTH.'

'But how can we?' wailed Sarah. 'And what
about Mummy and Daddy?'

'THE . . . BIG . . . GIANTS . . . WILL . . . NOT
. . . KNOW . . . YOU . . . HAVE . . . GONE . . .
AND . . . I . . . PROMISE . . . TO . . . BRING . . .
YOU . . . BACK . . . SAFELY.'

'But you said it took you a trillion dark years
to get here,' Sarah protested. 'We can't be away
all that time.'

'THERE . . . IS . . . NO . . . TIME . . . IN . . .
INNER . . . SPACE.'

'Would it hurt?' Rufus asked anxiously. 'If
we let you make us small, I mean.'

'NOTHING . . . WILL . . . HURT . . . YOU.'

'What do you think, Sarah. Shall we go?'

'Oh, yes! We don't want poor Zozu to be
scrapped, do we?'

'All right,' Rufus told the robot. 'We'll come
to plant six.'

Sarah asked, 'What do we have to do?'

'FIRST . . . CLIMB . . . ON . . . THE . . .
TABLE.'

Zozu disappeared into the matter machine
while Rufus gave Sarah a hand and then climbed
on to the table himself.

Then Zozu reappeared, carrying something that looked rather like a gun.

'Are you absolutely sure it won't hurt?' Rufus repeated.

'ABSOLUTELY,' said Zozu. 'WHO . . . SHALL . . . I . . . MAKE . . . SMALL . . . FIRST?'

'Me, me!' begged Sarah.

Zozu pointed his get-small machine at her foot and pulled the trigger. A beam of bright light shone on Sarah's ankle and she felt herself growing smaller and smaller and smaller.

When Sarah was the same height as himself, Zozu took his finger off the trigger of the get-small machine.

'What was it like?' Rufus asked Sarah.

She stared up at him.

'It didn't hurt,' she replied in a funny squeaky little voice. 'But you do look enormous. And you've got dirty toenails,' she added, prodding Rufus's foot with one of her tiny hands.

'Don't do that,' he snapped. 'It tickles. Do me now, Zozu.'

The robot pointed the get-small machine at Rufus and pulled the trigger again.

Unfortunately, at that very moment, Sarah decided to climb on to the pink hill that was Rufus's foot.

Poor Rufus!

As he began to get smaller, the tickling became

unbearable and, without thinking, he kicked the matter machine off the table. It fell to the floor with a thump.

'Oh, no!' shouted Sarah. 'Now look what you've done.'

Zozu turned bright green. He was so scared that he forgot to take his finger off the trigger of the get-small machine.

'Stop, Zozu!' shouted Rufus when he saw that he was the same size as Sarah.

But the seven fingers of Zozu's right hand were stiff with fright.

'Stop!' screamed Rufus.

Already Sarah looked as tall as her mother.

'I'll disappear completely in a minute. Do something, Sarah.'

His sister's hand closed over the robot's useless fingers and loosened them. The beam of bright light went out and Rufus stopped shrinking.

The top of his head just reached Sarah's knee.

'Golly,' she said, rather unnecessarily. 'Aren't you small?'

'Ha, ha,' said Rufus crossly.

'Can't you make him the same size as us?' Sarah asked the robot.

'I ... HAVE ... NO ... GET ... BIG ... MACHINE ... WITH ... ME,' said Zozu. 'BUT ... THERE ... WILL ... BE ... ONE ... ON ... PLANT ... SIX.'

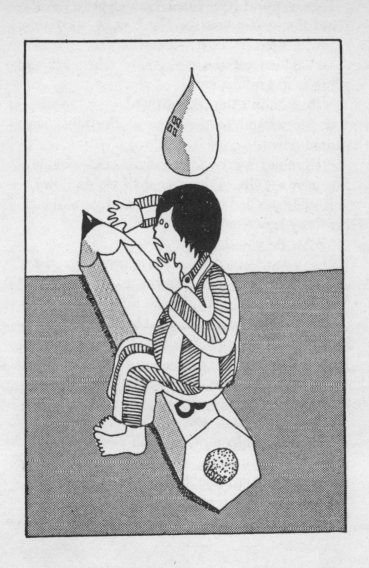

'Never mind about that,' said Rufus. 'What about the matter machine?'

'Well, what about it?' asked Sarah.

'It's fallen off the table, silly. How are we going to get into it now?'

'Oh. I hadn't thought of that.'

Sarah walked to the edge of the table and peered down.

'It's miles away. I feel dizzy just looking.' She gave a gulp. 'Whatever shall we do now?'

Rufus marched over to Zozu and gave one of his tinny legs a tap.

'What do you think?'

'I ... AM ... TOO ... FRIGHTENED ... TO ... THINK,' said the green robot.

'That's a great help, I must say.'

Rufus sat on the crayon he'd been using before lunch, put his head in his hands and thought hard.

Something warm and wet sloshed down the neck of his pyjama jacket.

He looked round and saw Sarah crying. Another huge teardrop hit him full in the face.

'It's no use turning on the waterworks,' said Rufus crossly, drying himself with his sleeve. 'You're the biggest now. Think of something.'

'I can't,' wailed Sarah. 'We're stuck!'

10

RUFUS thought again. Then, suddenly, he clapped his hands and smiled.

'Got it! What are we trying to find, Sarah?'

'A way of getting into Zozu's matter machine.'

'And that's a very difficult question, isn't it? So why doesn't Zozu pull that lever on his chest the one that makes the answer pop out of his mouth?'

'THAT ... IS ... A ... GOOD ... IDEA,' said the robot, already beginning to look a little less green.

'Rufus, you are clever,' said Sarah admiringly.

'Go on, Zozu,' ordered her brother. 'And cross fingers it works.'

'HOW ... CAN ... WE ... REACH ... THE ... MATTER ... MACHINE?' asked the robot, pulling the lever on his chest.

To Rufus and Sarah's great relief, a piece of paper immediately shot out of Zozu's mouth.

Now that Rufus was so small, the slip of paper seemed very large indeed. So, instead of picking it up, he walked round it until he could read the printing.

'It says, "Use get-small on table." '

'Of course,' exclaimed Sarah. 'Now why didn't we think of that?'

'Zozu?' asked Rufus doubtfully. 'Can you make the table shrink without us shrinking with it?'

'YES,' said the robot. 'ONLY . . THE . . . OBJECT . . . IN . . . THE . . . LIGHT . . . OF . . . THE . . . GET . . . SMALL . . . MACHINE . . . WILL . . . SHRINK.'

'That's good,' said Rufus.

Zozu pointed the get-small machine at the wood between his saucer-like feet.

'ARE . . . YOU . . . BOTH . . . READY?'

'Ready,' said Rufus and Sarah together.

'FIRE.'

The bright light shone on the tabletop and down and down it went with the children and the robot on it.

It felt, Sarah decided, like being in a lift.

And still the table grew smaller as the carpet came nearer and nearer.

Zozu took his finger off the trigger.

Then he and Sarah help Rufus on to the floor.

'Golly,' Rufus exclaimed, making swimming movements with his arms. 'I can hardly move. The carpet's like being in a field full of very tall grass.'

Sarah, being bigger, found walking much easier.

'Take my hand,' she said to poor Rufus who was puffiing and blowing as he struggled through the tufts towards the matter machine.

By the time Sarah and Zozu had pushed and pulled Rufus up the flight of steps, he was completely out of breath.

The robot beckoned the children inside the matter machine.

Both gasped as they stepped through the egg-shaped doorway

To their left, were row upon row of buttons, knobs, and switches, just like the ones on Zozu's chest. The right-hand side of the matter machine contained a beautiful curved rainbow, solid to the touch. Hidden machinery made beep-beep and buzz-buzz noises.

Three shimmering bubbles bobbed gently on the floor of the machine.

'Mister Pink!' Rufus gasped. 'Look, Sarah. He's in that bubble'.

His sister gave a shudder.

'Now I know why Zozu went all green when he saw him. Mister Pink does look frightening when he's as big as you are. His front teeth are huge!'

'Can't he get out?' Rufus asked the robot.

'NOT ... UNTIL ... I ... RELEASE ... HIM.'

'And what's that bristly thing curled up in the second bubble?' Sarah wanted to know.

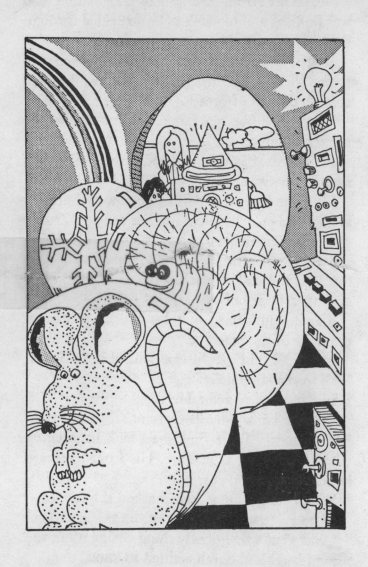

'The caterpillar,' said Rufus. 'I suppose it's asleep. 'And that,' he pointed to the third bubble, 'must be the potato peeling.'

'Where's the snow, Zozu?' asked Sarah.

In reply, the robot pushed so many buttons, turned so many knobs and pulled so many levers that she couldn't keep pace with his fourteen flying fingers.

Gradually, something grew and took shape between the two children. When it was complete they saw a single delicate snowflake, crisp and gleaming.

Then, before Rufus could reach out his hand to grasp it, the snowflake disappeared.

Zozu turned round.

'MIND ... YOUR ... FEET,' he told the children.

They stepped back hastily as the matter machine was filled with a glop, glop, glopping noise. A tiny bubble appeared where Sarah had been standing. It grew and grew until it nearly touched the curved ceiling.

'NOW,' said Zozu, clanking stiffly towards it, 'INSIDE ... PLEASE.'

His tiny knuckles rapped on the bubble and an opening appeared.

Obediently, Rufus and Sarah stepped into the bubble. The opening shut silently behind them.

'Rufus!' said Sarah in a panic. 'We're trapped just like Mister Pink. We can't get out.'

'HAVE ... NO ... FEAR,' said Zozu. 'I ... WILL ... RELEASE ... YOU ... WHEN ... WE ... REACH ... PLANT ... SIX.'

The matter machine was again filled with the glop, glop, glopping noise. Another bubble appeared and grew until it bobbed beside the one containing the children.

'TRUST ... ME ... LITTLE ... GIANTS,' said Zozu. 'YOU ... SEE ... I ... TOO ... WILL ... TRAVEL ... IN ... A ... BUBBLE.'

The robot was very busy indeed, working at the buttons, knobs, and switches. Gradually, the walls of the matter machine seemed to dissolve until, when they were completely transparent, Rufus and Sarah could see out into their bedroom.

'NOW ... WE ... ARE ... READY ... TO ... LEAVE,' said Zozu.

He clanked over to the empty bubble and, when an opening appeared, stepped stiffly inside.

'MAKE ... YOURSELVES ... COMFORTABLE,' he told the children, 'AND ... WATCH ... THE ... RAINBOW.'

Rufus and Sarah leaned into the skin of the bubble. It felt warm and soft and bouncy.

Zozu began to count backwards.

'SEVEN ... SIX ... FIVE ... FOUR ...'

With each number, a colour of the rainbow disappeared.

At seven, the violet.

At six, the indigo.

At five, the blue.

At four, the green.

'THREE ... TWO ... ONE ...'

Yellow, orange, and red followed.

'NOTHING!'

They were all plunged into total darkness.

11

THE children and Zozu were wafted through the things we call time and space and matter.

They journeyed forever but it took no time at all.

They travelled through nothing and yet through everything.

And then came the first glimmer of light, seen through a thick, grey fog.

Little by little the children could pick out the shape of something far beneath them.

'THAT ... IS ... PLANT ... SIX,' said Zozu.

As the matter machine descended, the dark shape below became bigger and bigger.

Rufus could see lumps and bumps on its surface. But there were no rivers or seas, no towns or trees; just browness. Plant six was the colour of mud.

Very gently, the matter machine landed in a kind of valley.

Sarah looked at the drab hills that surrounded them on all sides.

'Where is everybody?'

'WAIT,' instructed Zozu. 'THEY ... LIVE ... INSIDE ... PLANT ... SIX.'

Sure enough, the matter machine began to

move downwards again. It went right through the outer skin of plant six and suddenly both children blinked.

Everything, everywhere, was a brilliant, almost blinding white.

The matter machine came to a stop in an enormous cave with sparkling, shimmering walls.

'OUR ... BUBBLES ... WILL ... DISAPPEAR ... NOW,' said Zozu.

As mysteriously as they'd grown from the floor, the bubbles containing the children and the robot grew larger and larger until, with a final explosive GLOP, both burst.

Rufus noticed some strange objects approaching.

'What are they?' he asked Zozu.

'THOSE ... ARE ... THE ... MOLLY ... CODDLES ... OF ... PLANT ... SIX,' the robot explained.

The Molly Coddles looked very odd indeed to Rufus and Sarah.

They had no mouths, or noses, or eyes.

In fact all they seemed to be was a collection of ping-pong balls held together with thin pieces of wire. At the centre of each was a bigger ball which glowed.

All of a sudden, Sarah was frightened.

'Don't leave us, will you, Zozu?'

'I ... WILL ... COME ... WITH ... YOU,' he replied. 'ONLY ... I ... CAN ... TELL ... THE ... INHABITANTS ... OF ... PLANT ... SIX ... WHAT ... YOU ... SAY.'

The Molly Coddles were all round the matter machine now. Rufus and Sarah could hear them making twittering noises outside, like a flock of starlings gathering in a tree for the night.

Zozu pushed a button on his chest.

The door of the matter machine clicked open

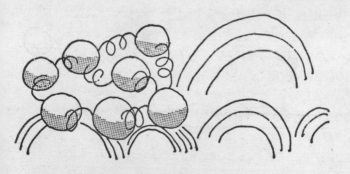

and the steps unfolded until the bottom one reached the shining floor of the cave.

Rufus and Sarah hung back. They were both nervous.

'LET ... ME ... GO ... FIRST,' said the robot, starting downwards on his stiff legs.

When the children had followed him, the Molly Coddles formed a twittering circle around them.

'THEY ... SAY ... YOU ... ARE ... A ... VERY ... STRANGE ... SHAPE,' Zozu announced.

'Tell them they look pretty funny to us,' pouted Sarah.

Zozu and the Molly Coddles twittered together for a while.

Then the robot said, 'NOW ... WE ... MUST ... GO ... AND ... SEE ... THE ... CLEVER ... CLONES ... BUT ... FIRST ... I ... MUST ... TELL ... YOU ... SOMETHING ... VERY ... IMPORTANT.'

'What is it?' Rufus asked.

'DO ... NOT ... TELL ... THE ... CLEVER ... CLONES ... THAT ... I ... CAN ... BE ... FRIGHTENED.'

'Why not?'

'BECAUSE ... THEY ... WOULD ... REPORT ... TO ... MY ... MASTERS ... AND ... I ... WOULD ... BE ... SCRAPPED.'

'How awful,' sympathized Sarah.

'EVEN ... MORE ... AWFUL ... THAN ... YOU ... THINK ... BECAUSE ... YOU ... WOULD ... BE ... ALL ... ALONE ... ON ... PLANT ... SIX.'

'Oh, no!' exclaimed Sarah, giving a little shiver. 'We don't want that to happen. We won't say a word, will we, Rufus?'

Her brother shook his head.

Zozu's tinny fingers closed round a big silver lever on his chest.

'AND ... IF ... THE ... WORST ... SHOULD ... HAPPEN ... PULL ... THIS.'

'All right,' said Rufus. 'We'll remember, Zozu.'

'AND ... NOW ... THE ... MOLLY ... CODDLES ... WILL ... CARRY ... US ... TO ... THE ... CLEVER ... CLONES.'

As Zozu spoke, the Molly Coddles split into three groups. One gathered round Rufus, one round Sarah and another round Zozu.

The children found themselves being carried along with their feet just clearing the white floor of the cave.

'This is nice,' Sarah shouted across to Rufus.

Faster and faster went the three groups, speeding towards a solid wall of gleaming white. When the Molly Coddles didn't slow down, Rufus braced himself for a crash.

71

But, just as he yelled, 'Watch out!' at the top of his lungs, the wall seemed to dissolve and they were in another cave, even bigger than the first.

The place was crowded with the strangest creatures Rufus could imagine.

Their bodies were rough and brown and from all directions trailed what he supposed were many arms and legs. In fact, though, they looked just like roots.

'THESE ... ARE ... THE ... CLEVER ... CLONES,' said Zozu. 'ONLY ... THE ... EYE ... IS ... MORE ... IMPORTANT ... THAN ... THEY ... ARE.'

'What eye?' Rufus wanted to know. 'Will we see that too?'

The faintest tinge of green started to creep up the robot's chest.

'II ... HHHOPE ... NNOT,' he stuttered.

12

THE Clever Clones surrounded Rufus and Sarah, rustling amongst themselves.

'What are they saying, Zozu?' demanded Rufus.

'THEY ... SAY ... YOU ... ARE ... NOT ... GIANTS ... AT ... ALL.'

'But they didn't see us before you used the get-small machine. Do they think you're telling fibs?'

'YES,' replied the robot. 'SO ... ONE ... OF ... THEM ... HAS ... GONE ... TO ... FETCH ... A ... REAL ... SIZE ... MACHINE.'

'You don't mean they're going to make us our real size in here?' said an alarmed Rufus. 'This place isn't big enough.'

'I ... HAVE ... TOLD ... THEM ... BUT ... THEY ... SAY ... SEEING ... IS ... BELIEVING.'

A Clever Clone, slightly bigger than the rest, arrived carrying a gun that looked exactly like the get-small machine in a different colour. As he passed Sarah, one of his trailing roots brushed her face.

'UGH!' she shuddered. 'He's all clammy.'

'You must try and stop them, Zozu,' Rufus said firmly.

Zozu rustled away, waving all fourteen fingers urgently towards the roof of the cave.

But it was no use.

The bigger Clever Clone simply curled out a root and flipped a switch on the robot's chest.

Zozu's lights went out. The feelers sprouting from the top of his head flopped lifelessly into his blank front eye. He could neither move nor speak.

'They've turned him off,' said an indignant Sarah. 'What a cheek.'

Making a horrible face at the bigger Clever Clone, she deliberately flipped the switch the other way.

There was a great deal of rustling and root-waving as the lights on the robot's chest flickered and then began to glow again.

'THANK . . . YOU,' he said creakily.

While Sarah's attention was distracted, the bigger Clever Clone pointed the real-size machine at Rufus. One of the tapering, wispy hands twirled round the trigger and pulled.

Instantly, Rufus began to grow. First he was level with Zozu and Sarah. Then he was looking down on the pair of them while his head rose steadily towards the roof.

Sarah spun round and tried to prise the machine away from the bigger Clever Clone. To her dismay, other wispy but surprisingly strong root-hands pulled her in the other direction.

As they struggled, Sarah heard a harsh ripping noise. At this, the bigger Clever Clone gave a sort of squawk and threw the real-size machine to the ground.

'Are you all right, Rufus?' shouted Sarah.

'I think so. Have I stopped growing?'

'Yes. Have you gone through the roof?'

'My eyes are still inside but the top of my head feels awfully cold and damp.'

'That's torn it,' said Sarah. Turning to the Clever Clones, she added sharply: 'And serve you jolly well right.'

But the Clever Clones ignored her. They had formed a circle around Zozu, rustling away like tons of tissue paper and waving their roots angrily.

Sarah could see that Zozu was just starting to go green.

The Clever Clones mustn't know about him being afraid, she thought. We don't want to lose Zozu now.

Sarah did the first thing that came to mind. She took a very deep breath, opened her mouth wide and uttered the most piercing scream she'd ever managed in her whole life.

The Clever Clones stopped rustling.

Encouraged, Sarah breathed again and screamed again.

'THEY ... WANT ... TO ... KNOW ... WHY

... YOU ... ARE ... MAKING ... THAT ... NOISE,' said Zozu, looking a little less green.

'Tell them to make my brother small,' Sarah panted. 'Otherwise, I'll go on and on and on like this.'

'What's happening?' boomed Rufus from way above her head. 'What are they doing to you? I can't bend my head to look down. It's stuck.'

'Zozu started to go green,' Sarah yelled. 'I'm trying to get you made small again.'

Zozu rustled at the Clever Clones, pointing at Sarah.

At last he said, 'THEY ... ARE ... BRINGING ... THE ... GET ... SMALL.'

'Sarah?' shouted Rufus. 'I'm getting pins and needles in my feet. I'll have to move in a minute and I don't want to tread on you or Zozu.'

Luckily, Sarah saw a Clever Clone slithering towards her with the machine.

'I'll take that,' she announced, snatching it out of his roots. 'I want to make sure Rufus is the right size this time.'

'Do hurry,' urged her brother.

'I've got the get-small machine and I'm pulling the trigger ... Now!'

Rufus shrank rapidly.

When she saw that he was the usual height, Sarah took her finger off the trigger.

'Oof,' exclaimed Rufus, rubbing his feet. 'That's better.'

'Oh, Rufus, you've no idea of how awful it was. They all rustled and wriggled their root things at Zozu until he started to go green. The only way I could think of stopping them was screaming.'

'You always were rather good at that,' grinned Rufus. 'Hey!' He pointed upwards. 'Take a look at that.'

Far, far above in the glistening white roof there was a big jagged tear. A bitterly cold wind blew through it. The children shivered in their thin pyjamas.

The Clever Clones felt it too. They hugged their rough brown bodies with their roots as if to try to warm them. As the wind howled and the cave grew colder, the Clever Clones seemed to shrivel. Then, while the children watched open-mouthed, their lumpy bodies developed ugly wrinkles. All at once, the Clever Clones looked very old.

'What's the matter with them?' Rufus asked Zozu.

'THEY ... CANNOT ... BEAR ... THE ... COLD.'

'Look!' exclaimed Sarah. 'They've fallen over.'

The Clever Clones lay all over the cave. Their

wispy roots were dry and withered, their shrunken bodies still. There wasn't a rustle to be heard.

'I'm glad,' Rufus gloated. 'I didn't like them. Anyway, if they'd believed Zozu was telling the truth, it wouldn't have happened.'

At that moment, they heard the voice.

13

'THIS,' growled a deep, deep voice which seemed to come from the very walls of the cave, 'is the Eye.'

Sarah and Rufus looked at each other in astonishment. 'Who's that?' they asked Zozu.

'THE ... EYE ... IS ... KING ... OF ... THIS ... PLANT,' said the robot. 'WHEN ... THE ... EYE ... DECIDES ... TO ... GROW ... THAT ... IS ... THE ... END ... OF ... THE ... BEGINNING.'

'I do wish you wouldn't talk in riddles,' snapped Sarah crossly. 'What do you mean, the end of the beginning?'

'THE ... TIME ... WILL ... COME ... WHEN ... THIS ... PLANT ... WILL ... MAKE ... WAY ... FOR ... OTHERS ... WHO ... WILL ... BE ... YOUNGER ... AND ... STRONGER ... FOR ... A ... TIME.'

'And then?' asked Rufus.

'A ... FEW ... WILL ... STAY ... IN ... THEIR ... PLACE ... AND ... OTHERS ... WILL ... VANISH ... INTO ... THE ... AWFUL ... UNKNOWN.'

'Why?' Sarah wanted to know.

But, before Zozu could reply, they heard the voice again.

'This is the Eye. Listen and obey, giants. I wish to see you. Now!'

Sarah frowned at Rufus.

'I don't like the sound of the Eye one little bit,' she decided.

'Poor old Zozu. Just look at him, Sarah.'

The robot had turned the greenest green the children had ever seen.

The Eye spoke again.

'Bring the frightened robot with you.'

At this, Zozu began to tremble so much that his tinny knees clanked together.

One enormous tear welled from his front eye and fell, splash, on to his chest.

Immediately there was a loud bang followed by a puff of smoke.

'Zozu.' Sarah gave him a little shake. 'What's the matter?'

With a great effort, wheezing and whirring, the robot managed to speak.

'B.L.O.W.N. . . . F.U.S.E.'

'What do we do now?' Sarah asked helplessly.

The Eye supplied the answer.

'He is only fit for the scrap heap. Leave him. I wish to see you.'

'Well, where are you?' demanded Rufus.

'Follow your noses, giants, and you will reach the Eye.'

Rufus grabbed hold of Zozu's stiff metal. fingers.

'Help me, Sarah. We can't leave him all on his own.'

Together, the children dragged the robot forwards, one supporting him on each side, while his shiny legs clanked uselessly on the ground.

The Eye laughed unpleasantly.

'You stupid giants. Why don't you leave him behind? He's no use to you now.'

'But he's our friend,' puffed Rufus.

'Robots have no friends but bring him if you must. Keep following your noses.'

As the children struggled onwards, they heard a roaring noise, like the sound you hear when you put a seashell to your ear.

The roaring became louder when they turned a corner and louder still when they turned another.

Rufus, Sarah and the lifeless robot were in a long tunnel which sloped up and up towards a pinpoint of brighter light.

'It isn't much further now,' said the Eye.

'I should jolly well hope not,' panted Sarah.

The pinpoint of light grew steadily bigger until, all at once, the ground disappeared from under the children's feet. It was such a shock that both let go of Zozu. The three of them slid and tumbled until they finally came to rest against an ugly black lump.

Looking around, the children saw that they had fallen into the centre of a white cave that was completely round. Its sides were smooth and shiny. No matter how hard they tried to scramble away from the lump, Rufus and Sarah kept sliding back again.

The lump felt warm and horribly squidgy.

In the middle of it was a huge green eye, fringed by pink lashes.

The way those eyelashes alternately reached out and cringed back reminded Rufus of a sea anemone he'd seen in a rock pool during their last summer holidays.

The great green eye rolled down to stare at the children and Zozu.

'I am the Eye.'

'Fancy that,' said Rufus boldly, trying not to show that he was scared.

'And this is Zozu,' Sarah announced shakily.

'Useless robot,' rumbled the Eye. 'I shall tell his master to scrap him.'

'Oh, please don't do that,' begged Rufus.

'And why not? He was sent to find the answer to the terrible question.'

'Well, he did try. Honestly,' said Sarah. 'And we came here to help him.'

'Help?' bellowed the Eye. 'You come here, make a hole in my skin, let in all the cold, kill my Clones . . . and you call *that* helping?'

'It wasn't our fault,' argued Rufus.

'Or Zozu's,' confirmed Sarah. 'He tried to tell those nasty rustly things what would happen.'

'And now you have the nerve to tell me you can answer the terrible question?'

The black lump heaved and rumbled, as if there was an angry beast inside it, trying to get out.

'You never know,' said Rufus. 'Why not try us?'

'Maybe I will,' the Eye mumbled. 'But first, I must arrange to scrap this silly robot.'

'In that case,' snapped Rufus. 'We shan't even try and help, shall we, Sarah?'

'No, we won't,' she echoed fiercely.

'Anyway,' said Rufus, 'Who are Zozu's masters? And where does he come from?'

'He didn't tell you?'

When the Eye laughed, as he did now, the black lump quaked.

'He said he came from earth.'

'Very well, we shall see how good you are at answers.' announced the Eye coldly.

Rufus and Sarah edged as far away from the black lump as the slippery floor would allow.

86

'Now,' said the Eye. 'Who farms fungus and keeps green cows?'

'Oh dear,' muttered Sarah, biting her lip. 'Another riddle.'

'Too hard?' rumbled the Eye. 'Then try this one. What builds a nest, flies for a little while and then tears off its own wings?'

'It doesn't sound like a bird,' frowned Rufus.

'It isn't a bird,' agreed the Eye. 'Think hard, giant. The robot's fate depends on your answer.'

Rufus screwed up his eyes and made a terrific effort.

Strangely, the only thing that came to mind was a hot summer day. He and Sarah were kneeling in their garden and watching something very extraordinary.

Then he remembered.

'Ants!' he shouted. 'We saw them flying and some did tear off their wings afterwards. Ants build nests too.'

'Well, well, well,' said the Eye. 'Perhaps you aren't as stupid as the robot after all.'

'But ants don't farm fungus and keep green cows,' objected Sarah.

'How else do you expect them to eat?' demanded the Eye.

Sarah scratched her head.

'I don't know, really. If you drop crumbs on a picnic, they carry them away.'

'I don't suppose they spend their whole lives just hanging around and waiting for picnics,' Rufus said sensibly. 'But I wouldn't have thought they were clever enough to have farms and cows.'

'Ants are a great deal more intelligent than you think,' boomed the Eye.

'And they made Zozu?' Rufus wanted to know. 'Just ordinary ants like the ones in our garden?'

'No ants are ordinary,' growled the Eye. 'And now that you have shown yourselves clever enough to save the robot, we shall see if you can answer the terrible question. Are you ready?'

14

Rufus looked at Sarah and she looked at him.

'Are you ready?' repeated the Eye.

Both children nodded.

'Then tell me about the things the robot brought back with him.'

'Well,' Rufus started doubtfully, 'he caught the caterpillar in our garden. And Mister Pink's our pet mouse.'

'Zozu went right to the top of the world to get the snowflake,' Sarah chimed in.

'Tell me about snow, giants.'

'It's white,' said Rufus.

'And cold,' supplied Sarah. 'If there's enough you can make a snowman or play snowballs. That's fun, isn't it, Rufus?'

'But what does it do to plants?' rumbled the Eye.

'Plants? Makes them cold, I suppose,' Rufus declared. 'But it doesn't hurt them as far as I know.'

Sarah thought of something her father had said last winter.

'Frost does,' she supplied.

'Aah,' boomed the Eye. 'Then why didn't the stupid robot bring frost?'

'Well, you can't pick it up or anything. It's just there.'

'Tell me about the caterpillar.'

'It sort of wanders around,' said Rufus thoughtfully, 'eating leaves and things until it's time to turn into a cocoon.'

'Later on it's a butterfly,' Sarah said.

'What sort of leaves does it eat?' asked the Eye.

'All sorts. Caterpillars that turn into white butterflies with black spots on their wings eat cabbage leaves.'

'Now tell me about the mouse.'

'Mister Pink? He lives in a cage in our room. Mummy says his cage stinks but we don't notice it, do we, Sarah?'

'Well, only a little bit if we forget to clean it out. Sometimes,' Sarah told the Eye, 'he gets into his wheel and runs round and round for ages.'

The squidgy black lump began to bulge and the Eye made a mumble grumble sound.

'Haven't you forgotten something?'

'I don't think so,' said Rufus.

The black lump bulged a bit more. Hastily, the children backed away from its sticky touch.

'What about the other bubble?' growled the Eye.

'Oh, that,' said Rufus airily. 'It didn't seem

worth mentioning. I don't know why Zozu
bothered to bring a silly old bit of potato peeling.'

The Eye rumbled more loudly than ever.

'And what is that?'

'It's nothing, really,' said Sarah. 'Just the
outside skin of a potato.'

'Just the outside skin of a potato?' echoed the
Eye menacingly.

'That's right.'

'And what,' demanded the Eye angrily, 'happens to the inside?'

'We eat it,' declared Sarah. 'Sometimes we
have it boiled. Sometimes we have it roasted.
Today we had it fried. Chips, you know,' she
added politely, in case the Eye had never had
any.

'I like them best baked in their jackets,' said
Rufus, smacking his lips. 'With lots of butter and
salt and pepper.'

'*How dare you?*'

The Eye sounded so furious and so loud that
Rufus and Sarah began to tremble.

'*How dare you boil and roast and fry and bake?*'

The squidgy black lump swelled again. The
pink tendrils that were the Eye's lashes reached
out graspingly to touch the children.

As Rufus and Sarah ducked to avoid them the
seashell roaring, which had only been a back-
ground murmur until now, filled their ears with

the sounds of surf pounding against a beach on a stormy day.

The black lump shook and shivered.

Slowly the huge green Eye opened wide, glinting with anger.

'Rufus, I'm frightened,' screamed Sarah. 'The Eye's going to do something terrible.'

Then Rufus saw something very strange. One moment the Eye seemed bright with fury. The next it was dull with pain.

The Eye groaned and its voice dropped to a whisper.

'I must tell the others. I must warn them.'

The Eye squeezed shut and, suddenly, the children were knocked flat by a great rush of wind. They heard a creaking, then a rasping, then a harsh rending noise.

Sarah was so terrified that she hid her face in the crook of her arm. But Rufus was watching.

He saw the black lump bulge and strain until it tore apart. He saw a small green spear thrust from the tear. It grew and grew, becoming a thick green column which reached the roof of the dome and burst through that too.

'What's happening?' wailed Sarah.

The Eye gave a pitiful moan.

'Spring. Too late. It is spring . . .'

The voice faded away.

The black lump and the Eye were gone. In

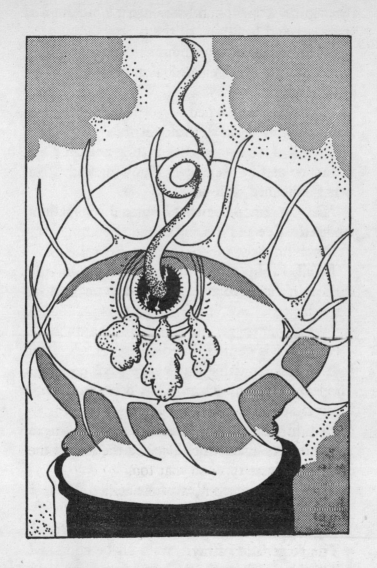

their place grew the green column which looked stronger and healthier all the time.

Rufus gave Sarah a nudge.

'It's all right. You can look now.'

She opened her eyes.

'Where's the Eye?'

'He's disappeared,' said Rufus. 'Is it my imagination, or is this place getting smaller?'

'It is getting smaller,' Sarah agreed. 'But what happened, Rufus?'

'Do you remember what Zozu said? Something about the Eye and the end of the beginning?'

Sarah nodded.

'Well, I think that's what happened. Only the Eye didn't *want* to grow. He had to because it's spring.'

'We'd better get out of here,' said Sarah. 'This place is getting tinier all the time.'

The circular walls of the cave were no longer slippery and shiny white. They'd become rough and yellow.

But the end of the tunnel, where they had all fallen to land against the black lump, still looked high and far away.

'We'll never reach it,' Rufus decided. 'Especially if we have to drag Zozu.'

'Oh, Rufus,' Sarah wailed. 'This is awful. If we don't get out of here, we'll all be squashed. It's the worst thing that's ever happened.'

Her brother's eyes opened wide.

'Of course! That was the other thing Zozu told us. If the worst happened, we were supposed to pull the big silver lever on his chest.'

Rufus leaned over the lifeless robot.

'Well,' he said, giving Sarah a rather crooked smile, 'here goes!'

15

RUFUS pulled the silver lever.

To Sarah's great delight, the robot's front eye lost its glazed look and the two feelers that sprouted from the top of his head sprang to quivering life. The green and red lights on Zozu's chest came on, one by one.

'WHERE ... AM ... I?' he asked, rather rustily.

'You're on plant six with us, remember?' said Rufus kindly.

Zozu stuttered, 'TTHE ... EYE ... WWANTED ... TTO ... SSEE ... MMME ... AND ... I ... BBLEW ... A ... FFUSE.'

'That's right,' confirmed Sarah.

'WWHAT ... HHAPPENED?'

'Well, the Eye told us to leave you in that cold cave with all the dead Clever Clones but we didn't like to do that so we dragged you here. Then the Eye asked us all kinds of questions.'

'WWEREN'T ... YOU ... FFRIGHTENED?'

'Terribly,' confessed Rufus. 'I had to sit on my hands to stop them shaking.'

'My legs were all jelly,' said Sarah.

'Especially when the Eye said he was going to tell your masters to scrap you,' Rufus added.

'Now, now,' soothed Sarah. 'There's no need

to go green. He didn't tell them. Rufus guessed the riddle.'

'YOU ... COULD ... STILL ... THINK ... EVEN ... THOUGH ... YOU ... WERE ... FRIGHTENED?'

Zozu sounded astonished.

'Well, we had to do something,' said Rufus. 'I mean you're our friend, aren't you?'

The robot's feelers became all tangled up as they always did when he didn't understand.

'WHAT ... IS ... FRIEND?'

'Well,' said Rufus thoughtfully. 'A friend's someone you like, someone you try to help.'

'Someone you share secrets with,' Sarah said.

'I ... THINK ... I ... AM ... BEGINNING ... TO ... UNDERSTAND.'

Zozu clanked stiffly to his saucer-like feet.

'AND ... NOW ... WE ... MUST ... GET ... OUT ... OF ... HERE ... AND ... FIND ... THE ... MATTER ... MACHINE ... QUICKLY.'

While they had been talking, the rough yellow walls had closed in even more.

Rufus eyed the entrance to the tunnel.

'Could you reach it if I lifted you?' he asked Sarah.

'Just about.'

Rufus grasped her round the knees and hoisted her body as high as he could manage.

'Any good?'

In reply, he felt Sarah slither out of his arms. When he looked up, she was kneeling in the tunnel entrance.

'If you give Zozu a boost up, I can pull the rest of the way,' said Sarah. 'But do hurry. The tunnel's getting smaller too.'

When the robot had joined Sarah, they both leaned down to give Rufus a hand.

The next bit was easy. The children and the robot found they could lie flat on their backs and slide down and round the tunnel as if it was a fairground helter-skelter.

They landed in the Clever Clones' cave which was already half the size it had been before and filled with a revolting, rotten smell.

All that remained of the Clever Clones were some brown stains on the floor.

'LOOK ... FOR ... THE ... REAL ... SIZE ... MACHINE,' instructed Zozu.

Sarah remembered roughly where the bigger Clever Clone had thrown it when Rufus became too big for the cave.

She pounced on it triumphantly.

'Well done,' congratulated Rufus.

Zozu was beckoning with one of his tinny fingers.

'THERE ... IS ... NO ... TIME ... TO ... LOSE,' he said 'THIS ... WAY.'

The robot clanked ahead while the children panted after him.

Just as Sarah felt she couldn't move her aching legs another inch, she saw the matter machine. But there was a sort of fence, made of ping-pong balls and wire, barring the way.

'IT . . . IS . . . THE . . . MOLLY . . . CODDLES,' said Zozu. 'THEY . . . HAVE . . . BANDED . . . TOGETHER . . . TO . . . STOP . . . US . . . ESCAPING.'

Rufus pushed against the fence.

'It's no good,' he puffed. 'We'll never get through. They're far too strong.'

Sarah looked around fearfully.

'If we stay here we'll get smothered by all that sticky yellow stuff. Think of something, Rufus. Hurry!'

But it was Zozu who solved the problem.

'HOW . . . DO . . . WE . . . GET . . . PAST . . . THE . . . MOLLY . . . CODDLES?' he asked aloud, pulling a lever on his chest.

As usual, in answer to a very difficult question, a piece of paper shot out of his slot-like mouth.

Rufus grabbed it.

'Use real size,' he read.

'GO . . . AHEAD,' Zozu told Sarah.

She pointed the machine at the fence and pulled the trigger. The fence vanished in the blink of an eye.

'Hurry!' shouted Rufus. 'Let's get in the matter machine before anything else happens.'

16

ONCE the three of them had trooped up the steps of the matter machine and the egg-shaped door had shut with the familiar click, Sarah gave a sigh of relief.

'Oof! I never thought we'd make it.'

Here, everything was exactly the same.

Mister Pink, the caterpillar, and the potato peeling were still enclosed in their bubbles. Hidden machinery made beep-beep and buzz-buzz noises. The curve of the rainbow glowed comfortingly and Zozu busied himself with the rows of buttons, knobs and switches.

'MIND . . . YOUR . . . FEET.'

Just as before, two more bubbles glop-glopped out of the floor. When Zozu made an opening in the larger one, Rufus and Sarah stepped happily inside.

Utterly exhausted, they sank into its soft and bouncy skin.

'NOW,' said Zozu. 'THERE . . . IS . . . SOME-THING . . . I . . . MUST . . . EXPLAIN.'

'Can't it wait till later?' asked Rufus anxiously.

Outside the transparent walls of the matter machine, he could see the yellow slime that surrounded them getting closer and closer.

'THAT ... IS ... PART ... OF ... WHAT ... I
... MUST ... EXPLAIN,' Zozu said.

'What is?' yawned Rufus.

'THERE ... IS ... NO ... LATER.'

'Huh?' exclaimed Rufus, suddenly wide
awake again.

'DO ... YOU ... REMEMBER ... I ... TOLD
... YOU ... THERE ... WAS ... NO ... TIME
... IN ... INNER ... SPACE?'

'Only sort of,' Rufus confessed. 'I didn't take
much notice.'

'WELL ... DO ... YOU ... REMEMBER ...
TELLING ... ME ... IT ... TOOK ... YOU ...
TEN ... MINUTES ... TO ... GET ... TO ...
SCHOOL?'

'Of course.'

'AND ... YOUR ... SISTER ... SAID ... IT
... TOOK ... HARDLY ... ANY ... TIME ...
AT ... ALL ... IN ... THE ... CAR.'

'That's right,' agreed Sarah.

'You laughed,' remembered Rufus.

'IF ... YOU ... WENT ... TO ... SCHOOL
... IN ... A ... MATTER ... MACHINE ... IT
... WOULD ... TAKE ... LESS ... THAN ...
NO ... TIME.'

'Less than no time?' echoed Sarah.

'Then,' muttered Rufus, thinking hard, 'we'd
be there before we left.'

'EXACTLY.'

'Do you mean,' said Rufus slowly, 'that we're going to arrive home before we've even come here?'

'THAT . . . IS . . . RIGHT.'

'But we'll see you again, Zozu, won't we?' pleaded Sarah.

'I . . . DOUBT . . . IT.'

'Why?' asked Rufus.

'MY . . . MASTERS . . . WILL . . . SCRAP . . . ME . . . BECAUSE . . . I . . . DID . . . NOT . . . ANSWER . . . THE . . . TERRIBLE . . . QUESTION . . . OF . . . PLANT . . . SIX.'

'But you did,' Rufus declared.

'I . . . DID?'

The robot sounded very surprised.

'How did he?' demanded Sarah.

'Don't you see? He brought us. We're the answer.'

'Us?'

'Oh, *girls*!' exclaimed Rufus, throwing up his hands. 'Where do you think we are, Sarah?'

'On plant six.'

'And what is plant six?'

Sarah looked puzzled.

'I haven't a clue.'

'It's a potato, of course.'

'A potato! We're in a potato?'

'That's right,' said Rufus. 'And what do people do with potatoes?'

'They eat them.'

Rufus grinned.

'That's the answer to the question. That's why potatoes disappear from the earth. We dig them up.'

'Oh,' said Sarah. 'No wonder the Eye got into such a temper about boiling, roasting, baking, and frying.'

'There you are,' Rufus said to Zozu. 'You see, mission one was a success after all.'

The robot went quite pink with pleasure.

'INSTEAD ... OF ... SCRAPPING ... ME ... MY ... MASTERS ... WILL ... SEND ... ME ... ON ... OTHER ... MISSIONS ... ALL ... THANKS ... TO ... YOU.'

'We didn't do much really,' said Rufus modestly.

'YOU ... DID ... SOMETHING ... EVEN ... MORE ... IMPORTANT ... THAN ... ANSWER-ING ... TIIE ... TERRIBLE ... QUESTION,' said Zozu.

'We did?'

Now it was Rufus's turn to sound surprised.

'YOU ... HAVE ... SHOWN ... ME ... TWO ... THINGS ... NO ... ROBOT ... FACTORY ... CAN ... MAKE.'

'What were they?'

'COURAGE ... AND ... FRIENDSHIP,' said Zozu. 'BECAUSE ... OF ... THEM ... I ...

WILL ... TRY ... TO ... VISIT ... YOU ...
AGAIN.'

'And take us on another adventure?' said
Sarah.

'I ... WILL ... DO ... MY ... BEST,' said
Zozu. 'NOW ... THERE ... IS ... ONE ... LAST
... THING ... I ... MUST ... TELL ... YOU.'

'Do hurry, Zozu. That yellow slime's getting
awfully close.'

'UNTIL ... I ... COME ... AGAIN ... YOU
... WILL ... FORGET ... ALL ... ABOUT ...
ME.'

'Never!' exclaimed Rufus. 'Forget you?'

'We couldn't possibly,' Sarah declared.

'YOU ... WILL ... FORGET ... ME ...
UNTIL ... I ... RETURN,' said Zozu. 'NOW ...
MAKE ... YOUSELVES ... COMFORTABLE ...
AND ... WATCH ... THE ... RAINBOW.'

He began to count backwards.

'SEVEN ... SIX ... FIVE ... FOUR ...'

With each number, a colour disappeared.

At seven, the violet.

At six, the indigo.

At five, the blue.

At four, the green.

'THREE ... TWO ... ONE ...'

Yellow, orange, and red followed.

'NOTHING!'

17

SARAH blinked.

She was in the room she shared with Rufus, snuggled under the bedclothes of the top bunk.

Her father was talking.

'Visitors from space might be very frightening,' he said. 'For instance, they could be huge giants.'

Sarah blinked again.

She had the funniest feeling that all this had happened before.

She even knew what her brother was going to say next.

'And they might be teeny weeny robots who were frightened of everyone except children,' added Rufus.

Those were the exact words.

Now her father would laugh and say, 'You could be right. Time you both went to sleep. Do you want me to shut the window?'

When he said just that, Sarah gulped.

At that very moment, a white ball decorated with red spots whooshed through the window, landed on the carpet, bounced twice, and rolled under the table.

'What on earth ...?' said the children's father, bending to pick it up. 'Is this the ball you lost?'

'That's the one,' said Rufus, grinning.

His father looked at the window.

'Someone must have found it and thrown it in. How kind of him. I'll put it away in the toy cupboard.'

'No, don't do that, Daddy. Leave it on the table where we can see it,' pleaded Rufus.

'All right. But take good care of it now. You might not be so lucky again. Good night, Rufus. Good night, Sarah. Sleep well.'

'Night, night, Daddy,' the children chorused, as he switched off the light and closed the door.

As soon as they were alone, Rufus whispered, 'Sarah?'

'Yes?'

'Have you ever had a funny feeling that something's happened before?'

'You mean you know what people are going to say before they say it?'

'That's exactly what I mean.'

'Did you have that feeling just now?' asked Sarah.

'Yes, I did,' said Rufus. 'It gave me goose pimples.'

'Me too,' confirmed Sarah.

She started to clamber out of the top bunk.

'Hang on a minute,' Rufus ordered. 'Wait till I turn on the light or you'll fall off the ladder. We've got to be very quiet.'

When they could see clearly, the children approached the table and stared at the ball.

'Something's stuck to it,' Sarah said, scratching with her fingernail. 'Ugh!'

She gave a shudder.

'It's a horrid, slimy bit of potato peeling.'

'And what's that caterpillar doing, crawling all over my big picture book?' said Rufus.

'Oh!' Sarah exclaimed. 'I've just remembered.'

'What's supposed to happen next, you mean?'

'No. That funny feeling's gone now.'

'So it has,' agreed Rufus. 'What did you remember, then?'

'Poor Mister Pink,' said Sarah, picking up the cage and looking at the white mouse huddled in one corner.

'We didn't give him anything to eat all day. He must be starving.'

'Well, give him that bit of fruit and nut chocolate you saved from yesterday.'

'All right,' said Sarah, smothering a big yawn.

Just looking at her made Rufus want to yawn too.

'Hurry up,' he said grumpily. 'I'm tired.'

A few minutes later, they were both fast asleep.

Seborga, Principality of the Roses, 1973